KT-479-274

ABERDEENSHIRE LIBRARIES

1947015

Note to parents, carers and teachers

Read it yourself is a series of modern stories, favourite characters and traditional tales written in a simple way for children who are learning to read. The books can be read independently or as part of a guided reading session.

Each book is carefully structured to include many high-frequency words vital for first reading. The sentences on each page are supported closely by pictures to help with understanding, and to offer lively details to talk about.

The books are graded into four levels that progressively introduce wider vocabulary and longer stories as a reader's ability and confidence grows.

Ideas for use

- Begin by looking through the book and talking about the pictures. Has your child heard this story before?

- Help your child with any words he does not know, either by helping him to sound them out or supplying them yourself.

- Developing readers can be concentrating so hard on the words that they sometimes don't fully grasp the meaning of what they're reading. Answering the puzzle questions at the end of the book will help with understanding.

For more information and advice on Read it yourself and book banding, visit **www.ladybird.com/readityourself**

Book
Band
5

Level 1 is ideal for children who have received some initial reading instruction. Each story is told very simply, using a small number of frequently repeated words.

Special features:

Opening pages introduce key story words

Peter Rabbit

Mr McGregor

Benjamin

Squirrel Nutkin

Lily

Mr Tod

Cotton-tail

radishes

6

7

Large, clear type

One day, Peter Rabbit and Benjamin went to look for radishes.

"Look out, Benjamin!" said Peter.

It was Mr McGregor!

Careful match between story and pictures

8

9

Educational Consultant: Geraldine Taylor
Book Banding Consultant: Kate Ruttle

A catalogue record for this book is available from the British Library

Peter Rabbit TV series imagery and text © Frederick Warne & Co. Ltd &
Silvergate PPL Ltd, 2013
Layout and design © Frederick Warne & Co. Ltd, 2014
The 'Peter Rabbit' TV series is based on the works of Beatrix Potter.
Peter Rabbit™ & Beatrix Potter™ Frederick Warne & Co.
Frederick Warne & Co is the owner of all rights, copyrights and trademarks
in the Beatrix Potter character names and illustrations
Text adapted by Ellen Philpott

Published by Ladybird Books Ltd
80 Strand, London, WC2R 0RL
A Penguin Company

001

Ladybird, Read It Yourself and the Ladybird Logo are registered or
unregistered trademarks of Ladybird Books Limited.

All rights reserved. No part of this publication may be reproduced,
stored in a retrieval system, or transmitted in any form or by any means,
electronic, mechanical, photocopying, recording or otherwise,
without the prior consent of the copyright owner.

ISBN: 978-0-72328-052-1

Printed in China

The Radish Robber

Based on the Peter Rabbit™
TV series

 Peter Rabbit

Benjamin

 Lily

 Cotton-tail

Mr McGregor

Squirrel Nutkin

Mr Tod

radishes

One day, Peter Rabbit and Benjamin went to look for radishes.

"Look out, Benjamin!" said Peter.

It was Mr McGregor!

9

"Run!" said Peter.

The two rabbits ran
from Mr McGregor.

They had three radishes.

Peter and Benjamin went back to Peter's house.

"Be good, you two!" said Peter's mum.

Peter and Benjamin
went to get Lily.

"We have three radishes,
Lily!" said Peter. "Come
and have them with us."

"One, two..." said Peter.
"We have lost a radish!"

"A robber has taken it!"
said Lily.

They went to
Squirrel Nutkin's tree.

"We can have the radishes
in the tree," said Peter.

"No you can't!" said
Squirrel Nutkin.

Peter went after
the radishes.

"One..." said Benjamin.
"We have lost a radish!"

"The robber has taken it,"
said Lily.

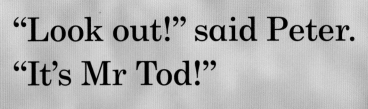

"Look out!" said Peter.
"It's Mr Tod!"

"Run!" said Lily.

23

"Come on!" said Peter.

The three rabbits ran and ran from Mr Tod.

"We have lost all the radishes!" said Benjamin.

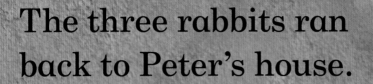

The three rabbits ran
back to Peter's house.

"Good," said Peter's mum.
"We can all have tea."

"Radishes!" said
Cotton-tail.

"Radishes?" said Peter.

"Cotton-tail got them for us," said Peter's mum.

"Cotton-tail!" said Peter. "YOU are the radish robber!"

How much do you remember about the story of Peter Rabbit: The Radish Robber? Answer these questions and find out!

- How many radishes do Peter and Benjamin have at the beginning?

- What do the rabbits do when they see Mr Tod?

- Who is the radish robber?

Look at the pictures from the story and say the order they should go in.

A

B

C

D

Answer: B, D, C, A.

Read it yourself with Ladybird

Tick the books you've read!

For children who are ready to take their first steps in reading.

Level 1

The Enormous Turnip ☐
Fairy Friends ☐
The Emperor's New Clothes ☐
Cinderella ☐
Goldilocks and the Three Bears ☐
Topsy and Tim Go to the Zoo ☐

Little Red Hen ☐
The Magic Porridge Pot ☐
Little Creatures ☐
Recycling Fun! ☐
The Princess and the Pea ☐
Rex the Big Dinosaur ☐
The Tale of Peter Rabbit ☐
The Three Billy Goats Gruff ☐

Why Giraffe has a Long Neck ☐
The Ugly Duckling ☐
Topsy and Tim At the Farm ☐
The Big Pancake ☐
Daddy Pig's Old Chair ☐
THE RADISH ROBBER ☐

For beginner readers who can read short, simple sentences with help.

Level 2

Beauty and the Beast ☐
Chicken Licken ☐
Rumpelstiltskin ☐
Sleeping Beauty ☐
The Gingerbread Man ☐
Dom's Dragon ☐

Little Red Riding Hood ☐
Nature Trail ☐
Sports Day ☐
Pirate School ☐
Sly Fox and Red Hen ☐
The Tale of Jemima Puddle-Duck ☐
The Three Little Pigs ☐
Why Lion ROARRRS! ☐

The Big Race ☐
Town Mouse and Country Mouse ☐
School Bus Trip ☐
Topsy and Tim Go to London ☐
The Princess and the Frog ☐
TREEHOUSE RESCUE ☐

 Available on the App Store

The Read it yourself with Ladybird app is now available

 ANDROID APP ON Google play

App also available on Android™ devices